NOW OPEN THE BOX

by Dorothy Kunhardt
author of "Junket is Nice"

The New York Review Children's Collection
New York

THIS IS A NEW YORK REVIEW BOOK
PUBLISHED BY THE NEW YORK REVIEW OF BOOKS
435 Hudson Street, New York, NY 10014
www.nyrb.com

Published by permission of Penk, Inc.

Library of Congress Cataloging-in-Publication Data

Kunhardt, Dorothy, 1901–1979, author, illustrator.
 Now open the box / by Dorothy Kunhardt.
    pages cm. — (New York Review Books children's collection)
 Summary: Although he knows no tricks, Peewee the circus dog is loved by all because
he is the smallest dog in the world, but when he grows into a normal-size dog his days
under the Big Top may be at an end.
 ISBN 978-1-59017-708-2 (hardback)
 [1. Circus—Fiction. 2. Dogs—Fiction. 3. Size—Fiction. 4. Growth—Fiction.] I. Title.
 PZ7.K94904No 2013
 [E]—dc23
                              2013015635

ISBN 978-1-59017-708-2

Cover design by Louise Fili Ltd.

Printed in the United States on acid-free paper.
10 9 8 7 6 5 4 3 2 1

Once there was a circus man with a quite tall red hat on his head and he had a circus of his very own so that was why he was called the circus man, and it was a wonderful wonderful wonderful circus.

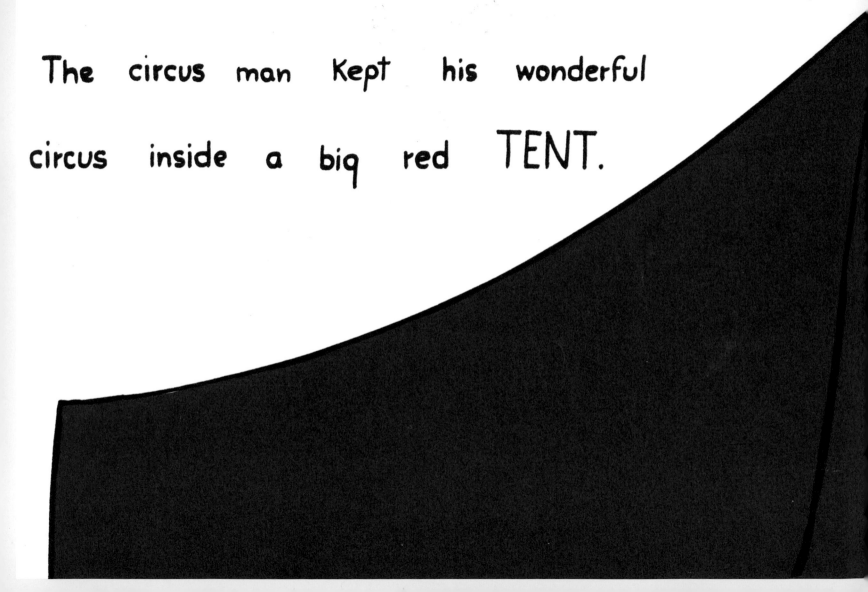

The circus man Kept his wonderful circus inside a big red TENT.

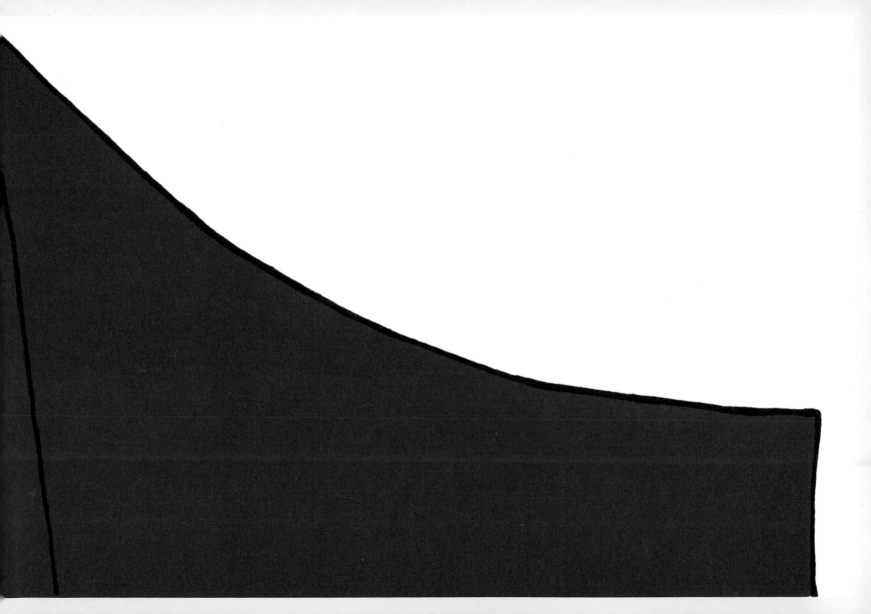

Every day the circus man stood in front of his big red tent and every day he held up something in his hand high up for everybody to see. He held up a teeny weeny little BOX in his hand and he shouted very LOUD ..... Come on everybody come on over here to my tent come on everybody I have something exciting to show you just wait till I show you what I have in this little BOX so

hurry up everybody and everybody came
running and skipping and hopping as fast as
they could to the circus man's big red Tent
and when everybody was there the circus man
said .... Everybody look now everybody look now
everybody LOOK now everybody LOOK !
Then he opened the box and out came

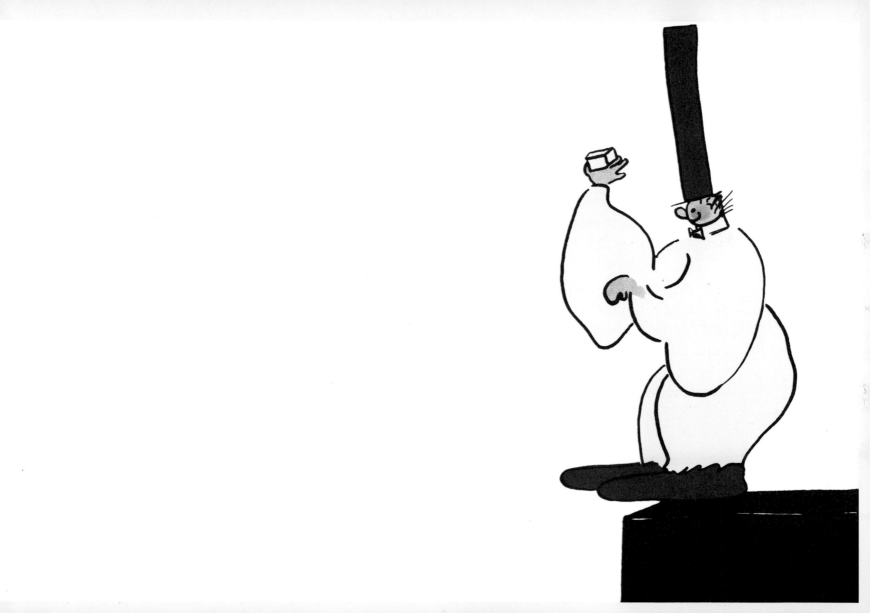

the teeniest weeniest teeny teeny teeny weeny weeny weeny little dog in all the world and he was dear little Peewee the circus dog. He just stepped out of his teeny weeny Box and he looked around at everybody and the minute he looked around at everybody everybody loved him. Then the circus man said Well I Knew everybody would love my little Peewee its too bad he doesnt Know any tricks not a single one not even how to roll over not even how to shake hands but never mind he is so teeny weeny that everybody loves him. And that was true because EVERYBODY loved little Peewee.

There was the clown riding on a donkey with two heads but one of them is probably make believe.

He loved little Peewee.

There was the fat lady. She loved little Peewee.

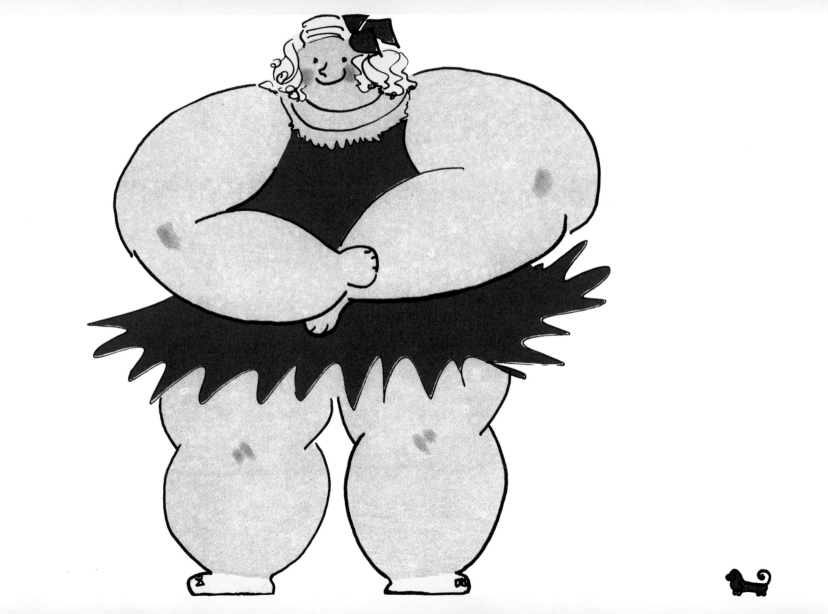

There was the man sitting on a chair on top of six tables just going to fall down and blowing soap bubbles. He loved little Peewee.

There was the lady standing on her head on an umbrella and with one foot she is holding a pair of scissors and with the other foot she is holding a cup full of nice warm milk. She loved little Peewee.

There was the elephant crawling
under another elephant. He loved
little Peewee.

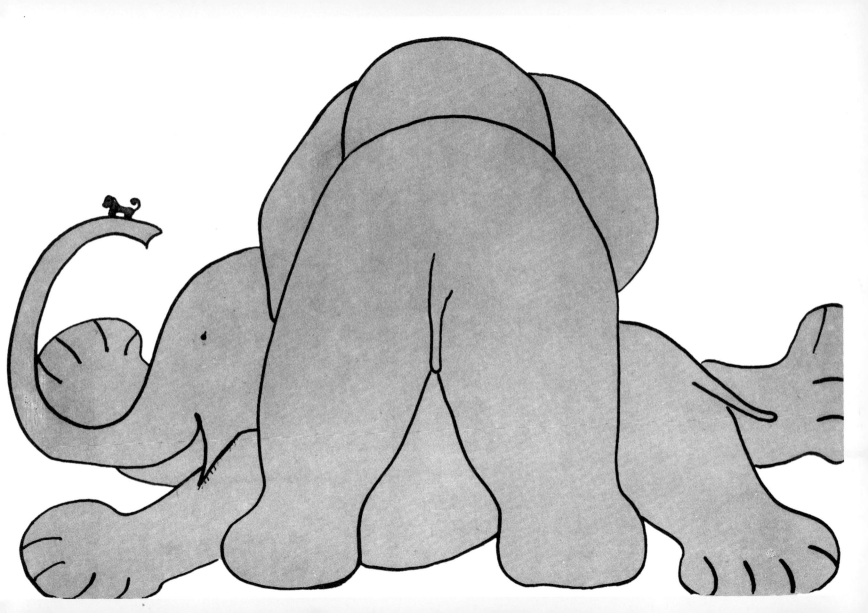

There was the thin man. He loved little Peewee.

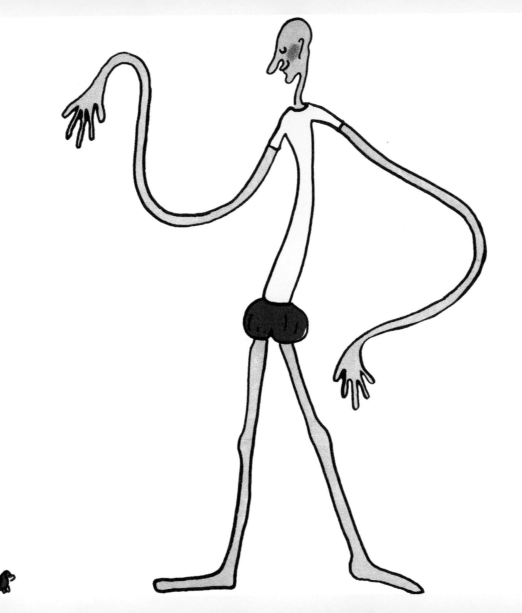

There was the strong baby holding up an automobile with a seal in the back seat. He loved little Peewee.

There was the snake that can put his tail in his mouth and then go rolling right up the stairs. He loved little Peewee.

There was the lady hanging in the air just by her nose being tied to a good strong rope. She loved little Peewee.

There was the giraffe who can swallow a big rubber ball without sneezing. He loved little Peewee.

There was the goat that can stand right on a bed with the bed all burning up and not even mind about the fire being hot. He loved little Peewee.

There was the huge tall giant.

He loved little Peewee.

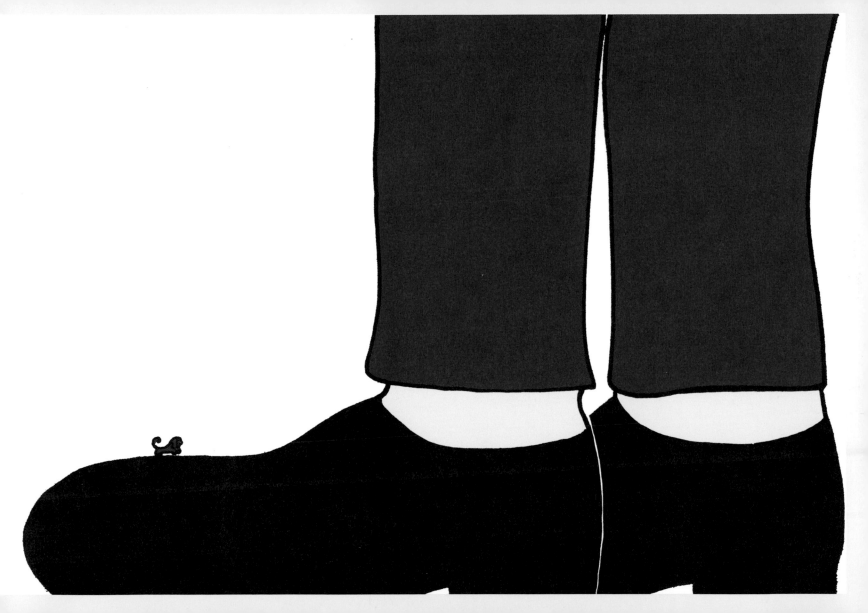

But one day a terrible frightful awful thing happened. One day little teeny weeny weeny weeny Peewee started to grow. And he grew

and he grew

and he grew

and   he   qrew , until

poor little Peewee the circus dog was just the same size as any other plain dog that you would see anywhere if you were looking at any plain dog and how could a circus man keep just a plain dog in his circus. Then the circus man cried and he said Now I can't keep you in my circus any more dear little Peewee and I am so sorry if only you could do some tricks it would be different but you can't do any tricks not even roll over not even shake hands and now you are just as big as any plain dog and how can I keep just a plain dog in my circus NO I just can't so we must say goodbye dear little Peewee.

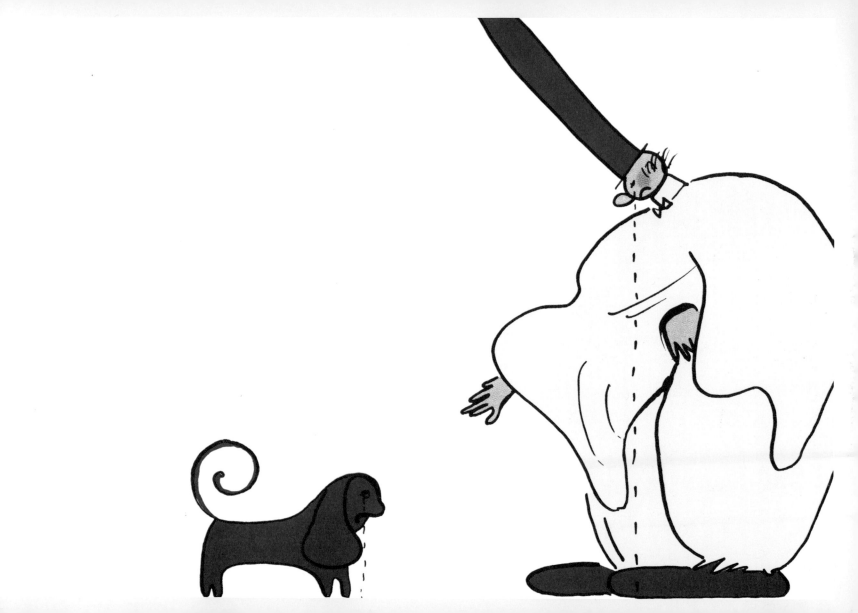

Then all the whole wonderful circus
cried and the whole circus said
Goodbye dear little Peewee.

So poor little Peewee started to go away and never come back to the circus any more and JUST THEN a wonderful splendid beautiful thing happened. Just as dear little Peewee was beginning to walk away so sadly and so slowly ..... he started to grow again! And he grew

and he grew

and he grew, and then

the circus man said Oh my dearest little Peewee now you won't have to go after all because now you are so lovely and big you are just the very dog for my circus! So little Peewee stayed in the circus man's wonderful circus and everybody loved him and every day

just before the circus started the circus man would stand outside the big red tent and beside him he would have a huge enormous BOX right beside him so everybody could see what a huge enormous BOX it was and then the circus man would shout Come on everybody Come on over here to my tent Hurry up everybody I have something exciting to show you Just wait till you see what I have in this great enormous BOX so Hurry up everybody. And everybody would come running and skipping and hopping to the circus man's wonderful circus tent and then the circus man would say Come on inside the tent everybody and I will open the BOX for you. And then everybody would help the circus man push and push the great enormous BOX into the Tent and then the circus man would open the top of the great enormous BOX and out would POP

dear little Peewee and the circus man
would say People this is my dear little
circus dog Peewee and he is the hugest
most enormous dog in the whole world
and I love him dearly and every time
the circus man said he is the hugest
most enormous dog in the whole world and
I love him dearly then little Peewee felt

VERY
HAPPY
INDEED!

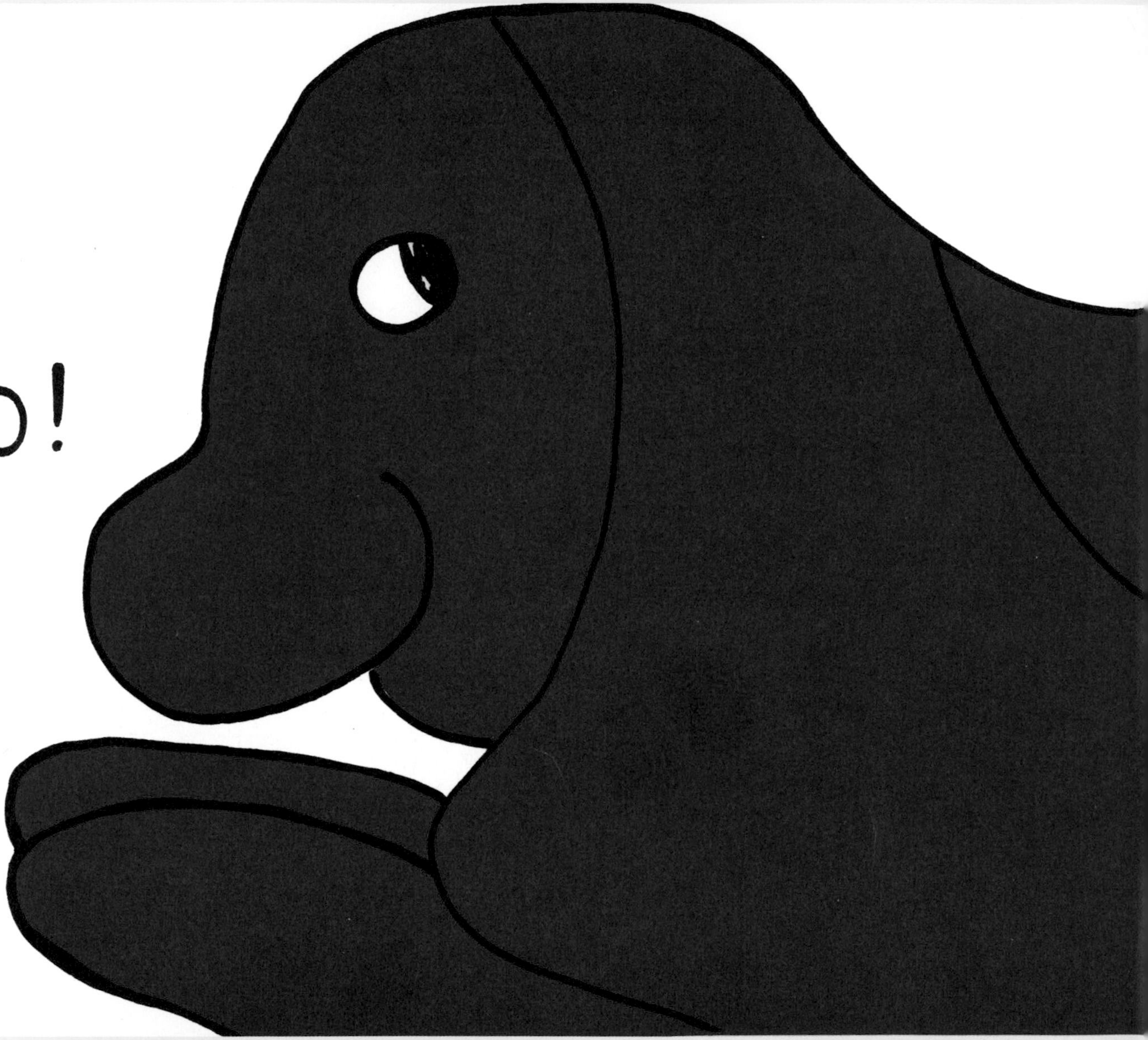

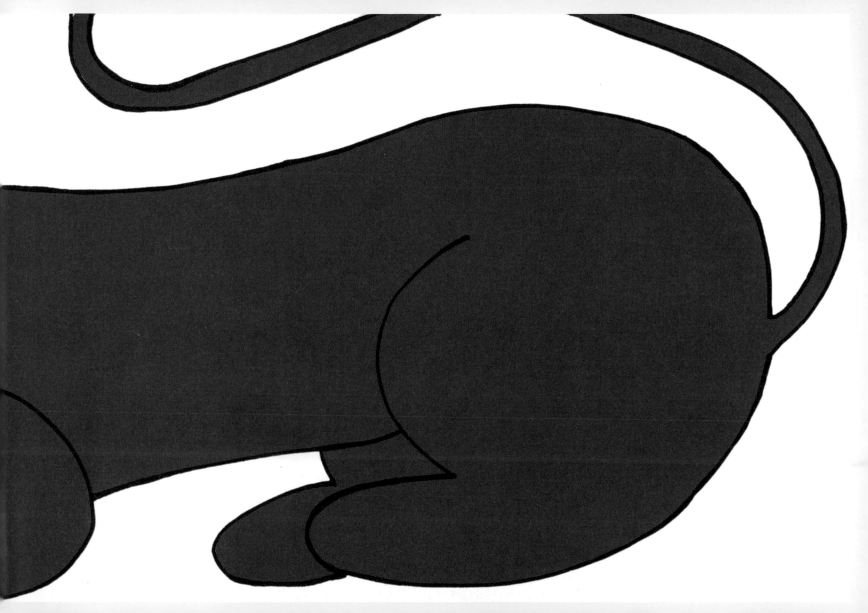

DOROTHY MESERVE KUNHARDT (1901–1979) was an American author of books for small children and is best known for *Pat the Bunny* (1940), one of the all-time best-selling children's books in the United States. Her first book, *Junket Is Nice* (which is also part of the The New York Review Children's Collection), was a success when it appeared in 1933 and was followed by *Now Open the Box, Lucky Mrs. Ticklefeather, Brave Mr. Buckingham,* and *Tiny Animal Stories.* Kunhardt published nearly fifty books, including several nonfiction works for adults about Abraham Lincoln and the Civil War (her father amassed a legendary collection of Civil War–era photographs and memorabilia). Several years after her death, Philip B. Kunhardt Jr. remembered his mother's boundless curiosity and appreciation for the way young people observe the world, writing in *The New York Times* that "for Dorothy Kunhardt a children's book was nothing more or less than a way to talk to children."

TITLES IN THE NEW YORK REVIEW CHILDREN'S COLLECTION

PENELOPE FARMER
Charlotte Sometimes

PAUL GALLICO
The Abandoned

RUMER GODDEN
An Episode of Sparrows
The Mousewife

LUCRETIA P. HALE
The Peterkin Papers

RUSSELL and LILLIAN HOBAN
The Sorely Trying Day

RUTH KRAUSS and MARC SIMONT
The Backward Day

DOROTHY KUNHARDT
Junket Is Nice
Now Open the Box

MUNRO LEAF and ROBERT LAWSON
Wee Gillis

RHODA LEVINE and EDWARD GOREY
He Was There from the Day We Moved In
Three Ladies Beside the Sea

BETTY JEAN LIFTON and EIKOH HOSOE
Taka-chan and I

NORMAN LINDSAY
The Magic Pudding

ERIC LINKLATER
The Wind on the Moon

J. P. MARTIN
Uncle
Uncle Cleans Up

JOHN MASEFIELD
The Box of Delights
The Midnight Folk

WILLIAM McCLEERY and WARREN CHAPPELL
Wolf Story

E. NESBIT
The House of Arden

DANIEL PINKWATER
Lizard Music

ALASTAIR REID and BOB GILL
Supposing…

ALASTAIR REID and BEN SHAHN
Ounce Dice Trice

BARBARA SLEIGH
Carbonel and Calidor
Carbonel: The King of the Cats
The Kingdom of Carbonel

E. C. SPYKMAN
Terrible, Horrible Edie

FRANK TASHLIN
The Bear That Wasn't

JAMES THURBER
The 13 Clocks
The Wonderful O

ALISON UTTLEY
A Traveller in Time

T. H. WHITE
Mistress Masham's Repose

MARJORIE WINSLOW and ERIK BLEGVAD
Mud Pies and Other Recipes

REINER ZIMNIK
The Bear and the People